Zuri and the Monster

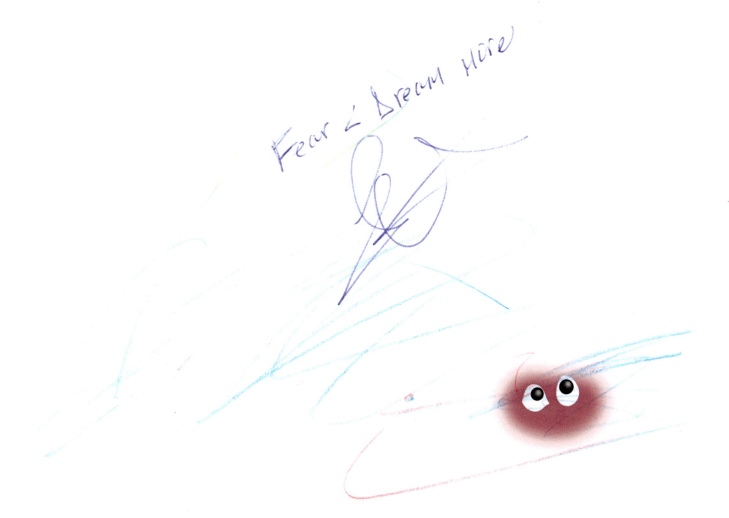

Fear & Dream Here

www.Tanishachambers.com

I would like to thank all my family and friends for their unconditional support and encouragement. This journey has not been easy in finding what I love to do.

I would like to thank Zuri for your daily creative activities and the joy that you bring into my life. Thanks Mom and Art, for always listening to my stories and the constant encouragement.

Thanks Rick and Sherrie for your great advice and mentoring me throughout this journey and figuring it out with me.
Thank you Kiera for stepping into be my editor when I needed.

"There is a story in each of us; it just hasn't been discovered yet"

- Tanisha M. Chambers

Bedtime was always Zuri's favorite time of the day.

After giving Zuri a bath, her mommy always read
a bedtime story that put her right to sleep.

But this night was different. Squeak!

Squeak!

Zuri jumped up after she heard a noise in her room.

She looked around, but could not see anything.

"Monster, Monster," Zuri called out. "Are you under my bed?"

"Monster, Monster," Zuri cried out again.
"Where could you be?"

Monster, Monster this is not funny!

Zuri finally got up and looked in her closet, but still no luck.

"Monster, Monster! Are you behind my door?"

"Monster, Monster! Are you behind my curtain?"

"Monster, Monster! Why are you scared of me?"

"Monster, Monster! Come out and play. My name is Zuri!"
"Monster, Monster! Please show me your face."

Zuri looked behind her toy chest in search of the monster, but still no luck.

Then she heard a noise come from her closet.
She jumped and slowly walked over.

Zuri smiled and told the Monster she wasn't afraid.
"Come out, come out," Zuri said.

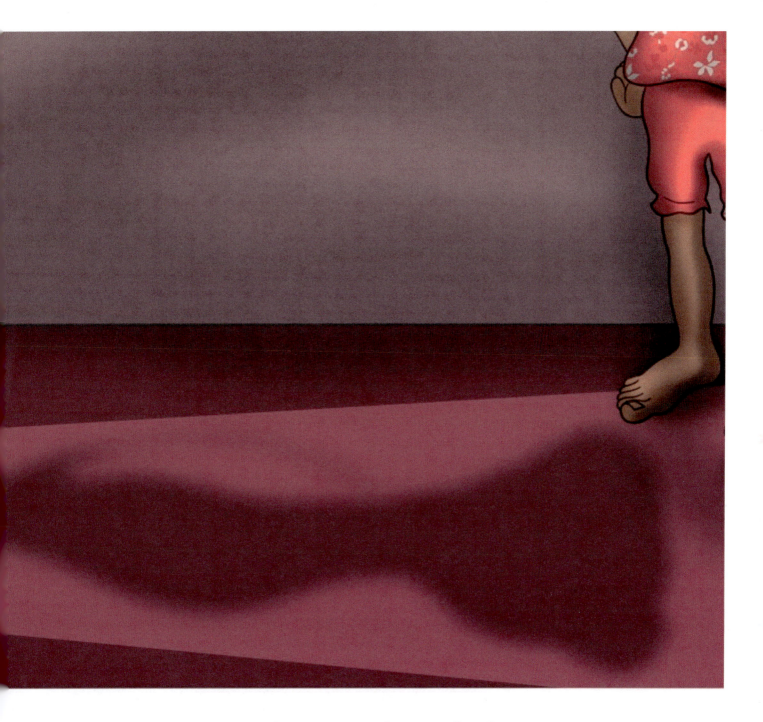

Zuri Then saw a huge shadow

The shadow Zuri saw started to become smaller and smaller.

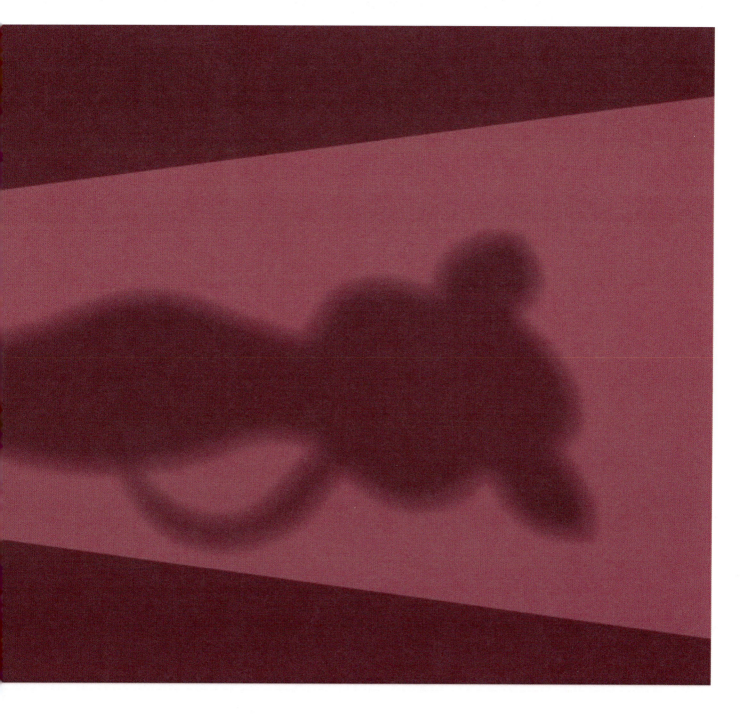

Suddenly, her kitten Kurly walked out of the closet.

Zuri picked up Kurly and got back into bed.
Goodnight Kurly. I'm happy that you weren't a monster.

Then Zuri finally fell asleep with Kurly in her arms.

Meet Zuri :)

Made in the USA
Middletown, DE
01 March 2024

50504243R00018